NUTTY KNUT

MARY ARRIGAN

POOLBEG

FOR CHILDREN

Published 1999 by
Poolbeg Press Ltd
123 Baldoyle Industrial Estate
Dublin 13, Ireland

Text & illustrations © Mary Arrigan 1999

The moral right of the author has been asserted.

The Arts Council
An Chomhairle Ealaíon

A catalogue record for this book is available from the British Library.

ISBN 1 85371 633 2

Illustrations by Mary Arrigan
Cover design by Artmark
Set by Poolbeg Group Services Ltd in Times 15/21
Printed by The Guernsey Press Ltd,
Vale, Guernsey, Channel Islands.

About the Author

Mary Arrigan was born in Newbridge, Co Kildare. She grew up devoted to her local library and reading everything she or her friend could borrow. Now, she lives in Co Tipperary and writes books for children.

She regularly reviews books for children for *The Sunday Tribune*. This is her first children's book for Poolbeg. She has contributed to a number of collections of short stories including *Scream!* and *First Times*.

To

Joe

Chapter One

Knut lived with his Ma and his Da in a longhouse with a thatched roof. Knut's Da, a Viking called Siggy the Big, owned a big farm beside a lake at the foot of a high mountain. All the workers and their families lived in huts around the farm.

Everyone said that the mountain reached up into the sky, but nobody had ever climbed up to see. They were afraid of the huge bird that swooped about away up there around the icy peak. Sometimes she swooped down to the farm, pinching meat that was roasting over the fire, or carrying off a whole basket of cooling bread. Everyone ran to hide whenever she was spotted heading towards the farm.

"You don't want to mess with that freaky bird," they warned one another.

Messing about with that freaky, scary bird was very low on Knut's list of things to do.

Knut was seven years old. He was small for his age. He never joined the other children when they played at being fierce Vikings, thumping each other with wooden swords and throwing toy spears at one another's knees.

"You'll be able to do all that stuff for real one day," Knut said. "Where's the fun in pretending? Why can't we play something just for laughs?"

"You're nuts," the boys replied. "Nutty Knut."

Every so often Knut's Da, Siggy the Big, set off with his men in a longship and sailed to distant places where they took stuff that didn't belong to them. This was called a raid and, when they came home, Siggy the Big and his men were always treated to a huge banquet of cabbage, peas, boiled meat, gritty bread and smelly fish.

"Welcome home from your brave raids, lads," the Viking women and children said as they searched through the stolen stuff to see if there was anything for them. There never was. It was always the same: sour wine and stinky leather.

"We had a fiercely great time," Siggy the Big would say, as he burped and held out his goblet for more sour wine. "We've shown those foreigners what a brave bunch we Vikings are. They're scared out of their tiny minds."

Knut thought this was a daft way of carrying on. He certainly didn't want to sail in a dragon-headed ship to strange places full of foreigners with funny accents. Besides, all those up-and-down waves made him throw up.

"Some day soon, Knut," his Da said to him, "you will come on a raid with me and find out what it's like to be a fierce Viking."

But that thought didn't exactly thrill Knut. What Knut liked most of all was to carve bowls out of hunks of wood. With his curved chisel he carved big bowls, little bowls,

bowls with fiddly decorations on them, bowls for drinking from and bowls for soaking the Vikings' smelly feet after a busy week's raiding. Knut liked to give bowls to people as gifts.

"It might come in useful," he'd say.

But the people in the Viking village were not very polite.

"Oh no," they'd groan. "Here comes Nutty Knut with another of his crummy bowls. The place is full of bowls."

The other children laughed at Knut and called him names.

"Yah! Nutty Knut," they jeered. "What good is carving soppy bowls?"

"Sissy stuff!"

"Knut the wimp!"

"Knut the nerd!"

"Ssshhh, here's his Ma."

Knut's Ma, Helga the Huge, was a big lady with two plaits and a hairy frock. She bossed Knut, Knut's Da and all the people in the Viking village. But especially Knut.

"Why can't you be like your Da," she'd say. "He sails off to foreign places and makes raids. You just mooch about carving those daft bowls. Get a life, son."

But Knut simply sighed and chiselled away at his bowls.

There was only one person who thought that Knut and his bowls were terrific. That was Freya, the blacksmith's daughter. She was even smaller than Knut and wore a long dress, a woolly hat and leather bootees.

"Don't you mind that lot," she said to Knut when the other children jeered him. "They're just a bunch of airheads. You are a craftsman, Knut. In hundreds of years' time people will dig up your bowls and say what a wonderful craftsman you were."

"Ta, Freya," said Knut. "You're a good pal."

Chapter Two

One day Knut's uncle, Olaf the Awful came to visit with his wife, Olga the Awesome. They lived at the other side of the lake. Olaf the Awful liked to boast that his raids were much better than the raids made by Knut's Da.

"Picked up some nice shiny loot last week," he said, flashing the gold rings on his pudgy fingers.

"Got me a grand bit of silk too," said Olga the Awesome. "Didn't you, my sweet little honeybun?" She held out a length of fabric to Knut's Ma. "Feel the smoothness," she said. "I'm going to have a really posh frock made with this."

"Hmmmpff," grunted Knut's Ma. "You'll freeze without your hairy frock."

"And smell the perfume," went on Olga the Awesome, putting her hand under the nose of Knut's Ma.

"Hmmmpff," grunted Knut's Ma. "I prefer the homey smell of salty fish myself."

"And what do you think of the velvet shoes?" asked Olga the Awesome, holding out a large foot on which a very tiny velvet shoe was stretched to its fullest. "They pinch like mad but, by golly, they're trendy."

Knut's Ma was really annoyed. She was pretty fed up with the sour wine and stinky leather that Siggy the Big always brought home from his raids. But she wouldn't let on to Olga the Awesome.

"My Siggy can get loads of gold if he

wants to," she sniffed. "He just doesn't bother with all that fancy stuff."

"Oh yeah?" scoffed Olga the Awesome.

"Certainly," went on Knut's Ma. "I bet my Siggy can bring back something much grander than your Olaf can."

"Ha!" laughed Olga the Awesome. "What do you bet?"

"I bet . . . I bet . . . " began Knut's Ma. She looked desperately around the longhouse and realised there was nothing here that she could bet. She swallowed hard.

"Go on, go on," teased Olga the Awesome. "Make me a bet."

Knut's Ma took a deep breath. "I bet our whole farm," she said.

There was a sudden silence in the longhouse. Knut looked up from the third bowl he was carving that day. What was Ma up to? Everyone knew that Da only ever brought back sour wine and stinky leather.

"The whole farm?" said Olga the Awesome.

Knut's Ma nodded with determination. "The whole farm," she said.

"Oh no, Helga the Huge!" groaned Knut's Da. "You daft nellie!"

"Oh good!" laughed Olaf the Awful. "I've always had my eye on this place. The view from here is really smashing and your beds are much more comfy."

"Poor Da," whispered Knut.

"Your Ma is a nutter," said Freya. "Siggy the Big and Olga the Awesome will lord it over us all and make our lives miserable. We'll be made to work ten times harder than we do and get less food, and moth-eaten blankets."

"My Da might just pull this off," said Knut loyally. "He might just bring back something grander than Olaf the Awful."

"Ha!" laughed Freya. "Fat chance. All

your Da ever brings back is sour wine and stinky leather."

They both looked over to where the grown-ups were still arguing.

"Tell them you were only kidding, my little sweetums," pleaded Knut's Da.

But Knut's Ma had made up her mind. She folded her great big arms and stuck out her chin. "A bet is a bet," she said. "And don't call me your little sweetums until you come back here with some classy stuff. I've had it up to here with sour wine and stinky leather."

Knut's Da groaned again and ran his fingers through his tangled hair.

"What's to become of us?" he wailed.

"I'll give you a fair chance," said Olaf the Awful. "I'll give you until a week from next Thor's Day. At sunset on that day, if your raid is not as good as mine, then I get to keep your farm, okay?"

"Okay," sighed Knut's Da. There was no getting out of this. A Viking bet must always be honoured.

"And what do we get when my Da comes back with something grand?" asked Knut.

12

"Good point, son," said his Da. "What's in this for me, Awful Olaf?"

"As if!" laughed Olaf the Awful. "But I'm a fair man. If you bring back something grander than I do, then you can have my magnificent longship."

"Hmmm," mused Siggy the Big. It was a tempting offer. His own longship was pretty leaky and there were holes in the sails. "Okay, done," he said to his brother.

Olaf the Awful laughed and winked at his wife as if to say that there was no way they were going to lose their longship in this bet.

"Darn it," said Knut to Freya. "If those two take over our place I'll have to kiss my bowls goodbye. Olga the Awesome will have me doing something rotten like chasing after squashy-nosed boars or fighting foreign people. That is, if I'm even allowed to stay. Probably not."

"Don't worry, Knut," said Freya. "Like you said, your Da just might come up with something."

But Knut knew she was just trying to console him. He knew that his Da was sure to lose everything. Unless, of course, something happened that would make him win the bet.

Chapter Three

Over the next few days the Viking village was very busy as Knut's Da, Siggy the Big, prepared to set sail on the big, important raid. The longship had all its holes patched and its sails darned. Freya's Da, Sven the Blacksmith, worked day and night hammering out battle-axes and swords on his big anvil. The children filled barrels with salty fish and tough, dried beef. Knut's Ma brushed the moths out of the furs that would keep her Siggy cosy on the seas at night. Bags of flour and barrels of water were stored along the middle of the longship.

Soon everything was aboard, ready for the big journey. The longship was rolled over logs down to the sea where it rose and fell with the waves. The men said goodbye to their wives and families, put on their metal helmets and jumped on board. Knut went over to where his Ma was hugging his Da.

"Bye, Da," said Knut.

"Actually it's 'Bye Ma'," said Helga the Huge. "Your Da and I have decided that it's time for you to learn to be a fierce Viking so here's a hairy shirt I weaved specially for you in honour of your first raid."

"What!" cried Knut. "I don't want to go on any stupid raid. Tell her, Da. Tell her I'm not ready yet. Besides, I'll probably throw up all over your good longship."

But Siggy the Big just shook his head. "Have to start sometime, lad," he said. "Might as well be now."

Knut looked helplessly at his best friend,

Freya, as his Da lifted him up into the dragon-headed longship.

"You'll be all right, Knut," called Freya. "I'll mind your bowls for you."

Knut wished that she could come too. It wouldn't be so bad if Freya was there to urge him along. But girls were not allowed on longships.

"Be a good lad," called Knut's Ma. "Thump lots of foreigners and bring back some classy stuff. Don't let your Da load up the longship with sour wine and stinky leather."

Knut looked back at Freya and Helga the Huge and the boys who wished *they* could have come on this raid. "I hate this," he said. "I really hate this."

The waves made the longship rise and fall, rise and fall. Knut ran to the side and threw up. Then he ran to the other side and threw up again. "I told you," he said to his Da. "I told you I'm not cut out for this lark."

"Don't be daft," said Siggy the Big. "We haven't even left the fjord yet. The men haven't even put their oars through the holes in the sides. Get real, son. This will be the adventure of a lifetime."

But Knut just groaned and tucked himself away in the smallest space at the very back of the longship.

Soon they were out on the open sea. The dragon's head bobbed and rose in the strong waves. Night-time came and Knut wrapped

18

himself in one of the furs, but it didn't keep out the cold.

"Grand fresh night breeze," said Siggy the Big. "We'll be on land in no time at all."

"Can't be soon enough for me," muttered Knut. "Where are we going, Da?"

"Ireland," said Siggy the Big. "I thought we might try Ireland. The pickings are supposed to be good there."

And so they sailed for several wet, windy, heaving days in the dragon-headed longship. Knut ate nothing but the odd dried apple and wished he was anywhere but here. After a few days the longship was smelly and very damp. No matter where he went on board, it was damp.

"I'll waste away and be just a damp lot of bones in a hairy shirt," he told his Da.

But Siggy the Big just laughed and clapped his little son on the shoulder. "We'll show them," he said. "We'll show Olaf the

Awful and his bossyboots of a wife that we're made of sterner stuff. We'll nick such a load of real fine stuff from these Irish that even Olga the Awful will be gobsmacked into silence."

"Yeah sure, Da," said Knut. "Dream on."

Chapter Four

"Land, Big Siggy!" shouted the lookout one breezy morning.

Knut pushed back the fur and looked out over the prow of the longship. Sure enough, away in the distance he could just make out a line of mountains that stood out against the sky. Land at last! Now maybe he could return to normal. He wondered if these Irish had good food. Something warm to thaw out his bones. His Da handed him a sword.

"Here, lad," he said with a touch of pride. "I had Sven run this up specially for you in honour of your first raid."

Knut took the sword. It was heavy. He hated the feel of it. He couldn't even thank his Da because that would be a lie.

"I can see that you're too overcome with emotion to thank me," went on Siggy the Big.

Knut put the sword in its scabbard and hung it from his belt.

"I'll actually have more use for my chisel," he muttered to himself, patting the curved chisel which was always tucked into his belt.

Siggy the Big and his men had never been to Ireland before. They stood with their axes and shields at the ready and looked at the miles and miles of green fields as the dragon-headed longship sailed up a wide river.

"There's nobody home," said the lookout. "Just lots of cows and sheep."

"Good," said Knut. "Now maybe we can go home, Da. No point in hanging about if there's nobody to rob."

"I promised your Ma that I'd pick up some classy stuff," said Siggy the Big. "If I don't she'll make my life miserable and, most of all, I'll lose my farm to my smartypants brother, Olaf the Awful."

Knut sighed. His Da was right. They'd *have* to find something classy before going home. But where would they find anything classy in all these green fields? It seemed quite hopeless.

Suddenly the lookout let out a cry.

"Some kind of a village ahead!" he called out excitedly.

The longship almost capsized there and then as everyone rushed to one side to see this village. Behind a circular wall there were several stone houses. Scattered around them were small, round wooden huts. Pigs and sheep grazed outside the wall. From one of the stone buildings there was the sound of lots of men chanting.

"Their singing is not up to much," said Knut. "We do a much better sort of song in Norway."

"Back, lads!" cried Siggy the Big.

But everyone was too excited to pay any heed to their leader. They pushed and shoved one another to catch their first glimpse of an Irish settlement. With a terrible creaking sound, the longship teetered for a moment and then slapped sideways into the water, throwing the fierce Vikings and their axes and shields into the cold river.

"Now look at what you've done, you stupid bunch of deadbeats!" spluttered Siggy the Big as he bobbed up and down in the icy water. "Here's a nice howdy-do!"

Knut swam for shore, his sword almost pulling him under several times. Two bald men wearing long frocks pulled him from the water.

"You poor lad," said one of them. "Come in and have a bowl of soup and dry those wet things."

Lots more bald men in long frocks came running down to the water's edge and pulled all the other Vikings ashore. Soon they were all sitting around a blazing fire in a stone house, their clothes strung on a line across the rafters. A big cauldron, with coloured stones set around the rim, hung over the fire. From it came the most delicious smell that

Knut had ever smelled. One of the bald men gave the contents a stir, tasted it and began to ladle it out into small bowls.

"Tell me," Siggy the Big said to the oldest man who seemed to be in charge, "whereabouts are we?"

"You're in a monastery," said the man in charge. "A holy place. We're all holy men," he went on, pointing to the rest of the bald men in long frocks who were serving the Vikings steaming bowls of hot soup.

"Mind your fingers on these bronze bowls," one of the monks was saying. "They get so hot they'd take the hands off you."

Sure enough the Vikings had to blow on their fingers after they raised the hot bowls to their lips.

"Try to look like tough men," Siggy the Big hissed. "We don't want this lot to think we're sissies."

Even though they were in their

underclothes, the Vikings had left on their horned helmets, just to show that they were still fierce warriors.

"I'm Knut and my Da is Siggy the Big," said Knut to the head man. "Who are you?"

"I'm the Abbot," smiled the head man. "And these chaps are monks."

"We're Vikings," went on Knut. "Ever heard of Vikings, Mister Abbot?"

"Heard of Vikings!" laughed the Abbot. "I've had it up to here with you lot. Raid, raid, raid. Don't you ever do anything else but raid?"

"You mean other Vikings have come here and pinched your stuff?" asked Siggy the Big.

"Certainly," replied the Abbot. "Chalices, really nicely written books, silver and gold crosses, genuine antiques, even the odd monk, all nicked by Vikings."

"If that's the case," said Knut, "why did you save us when our longship turned over? Why didn't you let us drown?"

"We're not into killing people," said the Abbot. "Besides, all those bodies floating around would pollute our river, you understand." He turned to Siggy the Big. "I suppose you'll be wanting to rob us now, when you've finished your soup?" he said.

"Well, that was the original idea," agreed Siggy the Big.

The Abbot sighed. "I'll get the lads to give you a hand," he said. "Just try not to bash the place about too much. We've just done a bit of decorating after the last lot."

"Hold on, Da," put in Knut. "How can we rob these nice people who have saved us, dried our clothes and fed us with the best soup and bread we've ever had? Have you no decency at all?"

Siggy the Big blushed under his shaggy beard. "I know all that, son," he said. "But you know the predicament I'm in. If I don't bring back something classy, we lose our farm. And your Ma will thump me and make life miserable for all of us."

"That sounds serious," said the Abbot.

"Mega-serious, Mister Abbot," said Knut. And so he told the Abbot about his Ma's daft bet and how his Da's life would be a misery from now on if they didn't pick up something classy on this raid.

"So you see," put in Siggy the Big. "I have to rob you or it will be curtains for me and my farm. We'll have no home and will have to wander through Norway, begging for a bite to eat and a shed to sleep in. Norwegians don't take kindly to that sort of thing, so we'll probably end up emigrating to some country that hasn't even been discovered yet."

The Abbot nodded his head in agreement. "That's a tough problem," he said.

"Still," continued Siggy the Big, "Knut is right. I'd never have another night's sleep if I robbed you and your nice chaps."

"I know!" said Knut. "We don't have to go through all that robbing stuff." He turned to the Abbot. "Why don't you *give* us something, Mister Abbot? Something classy that you don't use very much, and we'll *swap* something we have for it. That way you won't be robbed and we'll have what we want."

"Splendid idea, son," said the Abbot. "Your Da must be proud to have a brainy son like yourself."

But Siggy the Big was shaking his head. "Aren't you forgetting something?" he said. "Our longship has turned over and everything we had is now at the bottom of the river. All we have are the clothes on the line above and our swords. I don't suppose a sword or two would be any good to you, sir?" he asked the Abbot.

The Abbot shook his head. "Not our sort of thing, really," he said.

Knut glanced across to where the rest of the Vikings were finishing their third helpings of soup. Once more they were blowing on their fingers after each slurp. And suddenly a really wonderful idea came into his head.

"I have it!" he cried. "I know exactly what we can give you!"

Chapter Five

"Bowls!" shouted Knut.

"Excuse me?" said the Abbot.

"Those bronze bowls," went on Knut. "Every time you eat something hot from them, you burn your fingers."

"So?" said the Abbot. "Not a lot we can do about that, sonny, apart from sucking up our soup with straws. But the veggies tend to clog the holes, so we abandoned that idea."

"What you need are wooden bowls," put in Knut.

"Oh no," muttered Siggy the Big. "Give the bowls a rest, lad."

"But don't you see?" said Knut. "I'd have a full set of wooden bowls carved by the time you folks have the longship turned right way up again."

Realisation dawned on Siggy the Big. "Good on you, son," he said. "Wooden bowls it is." He turned to the Abbot. "My lad here carves the best bowls in all of Norway," he said. "He'll do you a neat line of kitchenware before you can say 'mushy peas'."

"Sounds good to me," smiled the Abbot. "And what would you like in return?"

"Something you don't use very often," said Knut. "We wouldn't want you going short on our account."

"Something with a bit of class," said Siggy the Big.

"How about a nice carved cross," said the Abbot, leading Knut and his Da over to the door. He pointed at a very tall stone cross which had all kinds of weird animals and little square people carved all over it.

"Hmmm, bit on the large side," said Siggy the Big. "It would probably sink my longship. Anyway I can't see my missus getting excited about a great hunk of stone like that. It has no shiny bits."

The Abbot scratched his bald head and looked around the big dining-room.

"Ah!" he cried. "How about that big cauldron, the one we made the soup in?"

"'But don't you need that yourselves?" asked Knut.

"Only when we have visitors," said the Abbot. "We like to impress callers like yourselves. Every other time we use a big bronze yoke that's black with age."

Siggy the Big and Knut went over to look at the big cauldron.

"It's certainly a fine big cauldron," said Siggy the Big.

"And these coloured bits of glass give it a nice touch of class," said Knut, pointing out the gems that were set around the rim.

"Your Ma would have to be impressed," went on his Da.

"Not to mention Olaf the Awful and Olga the Awesome," added Knut.

Siggy the Big smiled. "Done," he said. "We'll take the pot and give you wooden bowls. Fair exchange, eh?"

The Abbot nodded. "It's a deal," he said. "I wish all raids could be like this. Who knows, maybe a day will come when countries will do business like this with one another. A sort of common market."

Siggy the Big laughed. "What a daft idea," he said. "It will never catch on."

So, while the monks and the Vikings set about getting the longship right way up, Knut got some lumps of oak that had been cut for firewood and began carving a set of monks' bowls. He even had time to carve in some of the curly decorations and bizarre creatures that he saw on the stone cross.

"It's nice to have things matching," he said when the Abbot and his men marvelled at the new kitchenware.

"Clever lad," said the Abbot. "Some day, hundreds of years from now, people will dig up these bowls and say what a fine craftsman you were."

"That's for sure," agreed Knut, who had no doubt about his great talent.

"Why don't you stay on here for a bit, you and your lads?" the Abbot said to Siggy the Big. "See the sights. Have some craic."

Siggy the Big shook his head. "Love to," he said. "But we have to get back by Thor's Day or we lose all."

"Fair enough," said the Abbot. "A bet is a serious business."

The cauldron was scrubbed and scoured and stored safely on board. The monks gave sacks of special monk bread, green veggies, cheese with holes in it and barrels of buttermilk to the departing Vikings.

"Tell your friends not to call," shouted the Abbot as he and his monks stood at the river's edge to wave goodbye.

"Will do," replied Siggy the Big. "Cheerio and thanks for everything."

"And thanks for the bowls, Knut," said the

Abbot. "They'll save us a fortune on bandages for burnt fingers."

"Nice men," said Knut to his Da as they sailed up the river. "Pity about the draughty haircuts. Freya could knit them some trendy woolly hats."

The thought of Freya and home made him want to get this journey over with as quickly as possible.

Funnily enough, he didn't throw up on the return trip. In fact, he almost enjoyed it. Every so often Siggy the Big scratched his beard and looked at the big cauldron.

"Do you think your Ma will really like it, Knut?" he said. "Is it classy?"

"Of course it's classy, Da," replied Knut. "Believe me, I'm an expert on bowls and this one is far classier than anything in all of Norway. Besides being big and shiny, it has all those little coloured stones set into it."

"Hope you're right," muttered Siggy the Big.

Soon they passed the most northern part of Scotland and, after that, turned right for home.

It was on a clear, sunny Thor's Day morning that the boys on lookout on the hill saw them coming.

"They're here!" they shouted. "The brave raiders are back!"

Everyone in the Viking settlement came to welcome the raiders.

Knut felt like a real celebrity. People were asking questions all at once.

"Did you thump those foreigners?" asked someone.

"Er, um, well they'll never forget us, that's for sure," replied Siggy the Big. It was very important for Viking raiders to sound like tough men.

"That's right," chorused the rest of the

raiding party. "We showed them what Vikings are made of."

And what our underthings are made of, thought Knut. But he didn't say that out loud. It wouldn't have been loyal.

"My brave men," cried Helga the Huge, hugging Siggy the Big and Knut until their eyes popped. "And what have you brought? Something really classy?"

With great pomp and ceremony the covered cauldron was carried to a platform outside the longhouse.

"Stand back there, everyone," ordered Siggy the Big. "You don't want to be breathing all over our prize."

Everyone dutifully stood back. With his chest thrust out proudly and his horned helmet stuck down on his forehead, Siggy the Big whipped away the cover and revealed the monks' cauldron. The people gasped.

"It's big," they said.

"And shiny."

"And it has little coloured stones stuck in it."

"What is it?" asked Helga the Huge.

"It's a cauldron, Ma," said Knut.

"A cauldron," said his Ma, turning towards Siggy the Big. "You've brought me a big stewpot! You call this classy?"

"Yes, my sweet," replied Siggy the Big in a very small voice.

"You great big twit," yelled Helga the Huge. "I was expecting something like a nice gold crown or a few rings with seriously large jewels. And you bring me a pot! There goes the farm. We might as well pack our things and go. Olaf the Awful and Olga the Awesome will have a right snigger when they see this thing. Knut, start packing now. I don't want to be around when your aunt and uncle come to take the farm your Da has lost on us."

"Keep your hair on, Ma," said Knut. "We're not going to lose our farm. You have no idea what Da, and all of us, had to go through to get this classy cauldron. Big bald men, fierce-looking blokes, tried to roast us, took our clothes, pulled our longship out of the river . . . "

"True, missus," said the rest of the Vikings. "We're lucky to have got away with our lives. Only for the fact that we're brave and fierce, we'd have popped our clogs."

Siggy the Big winked at his son. But Helga was not so easily won over.

"Might have been just as well," she said. "At least it would save us a lot of embarrassment."

"Hold on, Knut's Ma," put in Freya, who'd been listening to all of this. "Let's ask my Da. He knows all about metal stuff. He'll know if this is classy."

"Good idea," said Siggy the Big, brightening up. "Everyone knows that Sven the Blacksmith is an expert on metal things. Send for Sven the Blacksmith!"

Freya skipped off and very soon returned, leading her big, brawny Da by the hand.

Sven never said much to anyone. But it was a well-known fact in the village that he was a very wise and very learned man. When he wasn't hammering things on his anvil he liked to think a lot. In fact he was so big into the whole thinking scene that he never noticed when his wife ran off with Erik the Goatherd three years ago, leaving him with little Freya to look after. Freya didn't mind her Da's hammering and thinking at all. She loved her Da. He never nagged.

Knut held his breath as Sven stepped up on the platform and examined the cauldron, inside and outside, top and bottom. Then he turned to the anxious crowd.

"This," he said, tapping the cauldron, "is the finest piece of metalwork I have ever seen."

A great cheer went up and even Helga the Huge smiled.

"It is made up of plates of gold, rivetted

together in a linear pattern to give it its splendid shape," went on Sven, getting quite excited. "It has been hand-tooled to perfection by craftsmen who, like myself, have the greatest respect for metal. The gems are precious rock crystals set in silver filigree . . ."

"That's all right, Sven," said Knut's Da. "All we wanted to know was if it's a classy piece of work or what."

"Don't you want to know about the inlay work and the bronze handles that have been fused on to the . . ."

"Grand, Sven," said Knut's Da. "It's just grand. Ta very much. You can go back to your anvil now, there's a good chap."

"There," said Freya proudly to Knut. "I told you my Da would know. He's the wisest man in all of Norway."

"Well, he's made my Ma happy," laughed

Knut. "Now she knows she has a classy thing, we'll all be able to breathe easy again."

"So, tell me, Knut," went on Freya. "What was it really like in Ireland?"

So Knut told her all about the bald men in frocks and how they traded together and became friends.

"Cool," said Freya.

"Yes, very cool," agreed Knut. "But you mustn't tell anyone. It has to be our secret." However, he knew that his secret was safe with Freya. She was, after all, his very best friend.

There was the smell of mutton being boiled. Cabbage and peas, which had been stewing for days were heated up again. Special bread, with hardly any gritty bits, fish that was only a week old and really pongy cheese were also on the menu. The sour wine was uncorked and, as an extra treat for this very successful raid, Helga the Huge had made a turnip mousse. The banquet for the returned raiders was about to begin.

Chapter Six

Servants rushed about, carrying platters and wine goblets. The long tables groaned under the weight of the food and the odd tired Viking raider who fell asleep on them. Siggy the Big and Helga the Huge sat at a special table at the top of the room. Some people danced, others sang and one or two argued over who was the bravest during the raid. A travelling poet recited some of his verses in a corner, but nobody listened. Except Sven, of course. He was fond of that kind of thing.

"Knut," said Siggy the Big. "Go out and keep an eye on that classy cauldron. We wouldn't want anything to happen to it after the way we risked our lives fighting off those bald men in frocks to get it."

Knut and Freya were only too glad to get away from the hot, noisy feast.

"Let's play hide and seek," said Freya. "I'll hide first. No peeking, mind."

Knut put his face in his hands and, like the honest boy he was, didn't peek.

"Here I come," he called, when he considered Freya had had enough time to hide. He looked behind the animal house. He looked inside the storage hut. He looked inside the pigsty. No Freya. Then he heard a giggle. It was coming from somewhere near the cauldron. "Ha!" laughed Knut. "Gotcha!"

But, as he turned towards the cauldron, an enormous shadow spread over the whole Viking settlement. Knut gasped when he looked up and saw the big bird from the mountain swoop overhead. Before he could even duck out of sight, the bird swept up the cauldron and carried it high into the air. Knut just had time to see his very best friend, Freya, waving frantically from the cauldron as it sailed away up the mountain.

"Oh cripes!" muttered Knut. "This is bad news indeed."

"Help me, Knut!" Freya's voice called out from the sky. "Save me!"

Knut watched helplessly for a moment before running into the banquet hall where the celebrations were still in full swing.

"Come quickly!" he shouted above the din. "Freya's gone!"

At first nobody paid any attention.

"Freya's gone!" shouted Knut again. "And so is the cauldron!"

At that everything stopped. Siggy the big's mouth opened very wide. So did his eyes. "What are you saying, lad?" he roared.

"Freya is . . . " began Knut.

"The cauldron, boy. The cauldron," went on Siggy the Big. "What are you saying about the cauldron?"

Knut gulped. "Freya has been carried off in the cauldron. The big bird from the

52

mountain swooped down and carried them both away."

Siggy the Big sank down onto his chair, totally gobsmacked.

"I'm totally gobsmacked," he said. "Please tell me this is a joke."

"No joke, Da," said Knut. "Freya was hiding in the cauldron when the big bird from the mountain carried them both away."

Everyone then rushed outside and stopped dead when they saw the empty platform where the cauldron had been.

"Oh no!" groaned Siggy the Big. "What will we do now? At sunset this evening Olaf the Awful and Olga the Awesome will be arriving here and we'll have no cauldron. All is lost."

"We'll tell them," said Knut's Ma. "We'll describe the beautiful cauldron to them."

Siggy the Big cocked an eyebrow. "Yes, Huge Helga," he said sarcastically. "They're bound to believe us, aren't they? My dear, they will laugh hysterically as they move their crummy furniture into *our* longhouse."

"Hey, what about my Freya?" put in Sven. "Has everyone forgotten that my little girl is up there with that big bird?"

"What?" said Helga the Huge. "Freya? Oh, yes. Freya." She turned towards Knut and frowned a very deep and meaningful frown. "It's all your fault," she said.

"Huh?" said Knut.

"You were told to keep and eye on that cauldron. How could you let that thieving bird make off with it like that?"

"And Freya," put in Sven.

"And Freya," added Helga the Huge.

Suddenly everyone turned and wagged their fingers at Knut.

"All your fault," they said.

"Little wimp."

"Nutty Knut."

"Should be ashamed."

"We'll all be ruined."

"Everything is lost."

"And Freya too."

"Wimp."

"Nutter."

Knut could take no more of this. He ran as fast as he could to the grove of trees at the foot of the mountain. There he sat down and put his head in his hands. He had never felt so miserable in all his life. *The villagers are right,* he thought. *I've let everyone down, especially my Da and my Ma. Now they'll lose the farm and the dreaded Olaf and Olga will take over. But most of all,* he sobbed, *most of all my very best friend Freya is up there on the mountain in the clutches of that enormous bird.* With that thought, he looked up at the high mountain. Its peak was hidden under the clouds. Somewhere up there was Freya, probably crying out for help. He would probably never see her again. He gave a very deep sigh and wished he could start the day all over again. But life doesn't work like that. One thing was for sure, he daren't show his face in his own village. He stood up, looked up at the high mountain again and made an enormous decision.

"I'll go up there," he said out loud. "I'll go up there and rescue Freya and get that cauldron. I'll go right now."

So, with his chisel tucked into his belt, his new sword in its scabbard and his Viking helmet firmly on his head, Knut set off up the scary mountain.

Chapter Seven

Halfway up the mountain, Knut looked down and saw the tiny farm way below. He caught his breath. Being so high made him very scared.

"Oops," he said. "Perhaps I was a bit hasty." But then he remembered Freya and her cries as she was carried off. And he remembered the awful things that would happen if the farm fell to Olaf the Awful and Olga the Awesome. Everything depended on him. He tried to muster up a bit of courage with that thought. Courage was scarce just then, but he took a deep breath and headed on up the mountain anyway.

"I wonder if they miss me," said Knut to himself. Then he shook his head. "Nah," he said. "They're too busy worrying about that stupid cauldron."

It was lonely up the mountain. Knut wished that Freya was with him. Well, she was, sort of. But she was way up at the top. *If,* Knut gulped at the thought, *if she hadn't already been a light lunch for the big bird.*

Up and up he climbed, trying to think of positive things like getting Freya back and hearing her tell him how wonderful he was, and trying not to think of bad things like falling off the mountain or being dessert for the big bird. The dessert bit tended to take over his mind, especially when he came to the part of the mountain that was hidden above the clouds. Nobody had ever been up this high before.

"Except me," Knut said to himself. He didn't know whether to feel really proud or scared to death. He looked down. There was nothing to see only cloud.

"I've climbed right outside the world," said Knut, his breath forming a freezing cloud as he spoke.

After a while he came to a really rough outcrop of rock and there, perched on the very edge, was an enormous nest. Knut was so awestruck by the size of the nest that he almost lost his footing.

"Cor!" he said, his voice echoing around the high mountain.

Just then a small head with a woolly hat on top appeared over the top.

"Freya!" cried Knut. "Is that you, Freya?"

"Of course it's me," came the reply. Who else did you think would be stuck up here in this freezing place? Are you coming up to get me or what?"

"Where's the big bird?" shouted Knut. First rule, always find out where the enemy is before barging into its territory.

"Don't know," Freya called back. "I'm baby-sitting. Are you going to stand there shouting all day, or are you going to get me out of here?"

With a lot of puffing and slipping, Knut finally reached the outcrop. Very gingerly he made his way along the rocky ledge until he reached the nest and peered in.

"By Thor's hatchet!" he exclaimed. "What are you doing, Freya?"

Freya looked up at him from the nest. There were downy feathers in her hair and stuck to her dress. She had a bundle of twigs in one hand, making a sort of a broom.

"What does it look like I'm doing?" she said. "I figured if I'm to be stuck here for a while I might as well clean up this place. It's a right mess."

Four large chicks twittered loudly on the other side of the nest. Four of the ugliest creatures Knut had ever seen, even in nightmares.

"I'm minding them," went on Freya. "Or maybe they're minding me, I'm not too sure."

It was only then that Knut got the most awful shock. "Where's the cauldron?" he cried. "Where's my Da's cauldron? It's not here!"

Chapter Eight

No sooner had he said those shocking words than a big shadow covered the nest. Knut looked up and saw the big bird, even bigger now in close-up, swooping down from the peak. In her claws she held the precious cauldron. Knut got so excited he totally forgot to be scared.

"Hey!" he cried. "What do you think you're doing with my Da's cauldron? Big thief!"

The big bird lowered the cauldron, which was full of water, into the nest. She frowned at Knut.

"Not that it's any of your business, sunshine," she said. "But I've been looking for something like this for ages. It's just right for giving my pretty little babies a drink of water. Except for the silly little jewel bits that stick out and get in the way."

"But it belongs to my Da!" exclaimed Knut.

"So, let him go on one of his tatty little raids and get another one," replied the big bird. "Now, run along, laddie."

"No!" said Knut, stamping his foot on the ledge. "You don't understand. I *have* to get this cauldron back."

"Sorry," said the big bird, watching the chicks slurp happily from the gold cauldron. "This time every evening I give my babies a drink for the night."

"Oh no!" cried Knut. "Time! I'd forgotten about the time! Olaf the Awful and Olga the

Awesome will be arriving at the village when the sun sinks out of sight. Listen, great bird, you simply must give me the cauldron."

"You tell her, Knut," put in Freya. "Tell her what will happen to all of us if we don't get that cauldron back to the village before sunsink."

And so Knut told the big bird the sorry tale about the daft bet and the loss of the farm.

The big bird listened patiently until Knut had finished. Then she shook her big, feathery head.

"Tough, lad," she said. "But as a loving, caring Mum, my chicks come first. If there was something else for them to drink from then everything would be hunky-dory. But, look around you. All that's up this end of the mountain is a load of old trees that were knocked down during the last land-slide."

Knut and Freya looked over the side of the nest. Sure enough, scattered below them were broken, uprooted trees. There was nothing that the chicks could drink from.

Suddenly Freya got very excited. She shook Knut's arm.

"Bowls!" she cried.

"What?" said Knut and the big bird together.

"Bowls," said Freya again. "Knut, you have your chisel. There's oodles of wood down there below us. You could carve a big bowl for the chicks to drink from."

Knut's face brightened. "You're absolutely right, Freya," he said. He turned to the big bird. "Would that do you, big bird?" he asked. "A wooden bowl?"

The big bird shrugged her great wings. "So long as it holds water, that's fine by me," she said. "If you can do it."

"Do it!" yelled Freya, now really excited. "Knut carves the best bowls in all of Norway."

"That's true," admitted Knut. "In fact, some day, hundreds of years from now, people will dig up my bowls and . . . "

"Yes, yes, Knut," said Freya impatiently. "Let's go. There isn't a second to lose if we've to get back down the mountain before the sun sinks."

With that, Knut and Freya hopped out of the big nest and made their way down to where the fallen trees were scattered. With his new sword Knut chopped a big ring of wood from the middle of one of them. Then, taking his chisel and using a stone as a mallet, he began to carve the biggest bowl he'd made yet.

Every now and then he looked up at the sun.

"I wish that sun would stand still," he said.

But the sun didn't stand still. By the time Knut was only halfway through, it was below the peak of the mountain.

"I'll never make it," he groaned. "I simply won't get it done in time."

"Stop moaning and keep carving," said Freya.

The only sound to be heard was the frantic tap-tap as Knut hammered away at the big hunk of wood. Finally he put down his chisel and stood up.

"That's it," he said. "What about some nice curly bits like I did in Ireland."

"Never mind the curly bits," said Freya. "Let's get this up to the nest. We might still make it in time."

But it was only a big might. The sun was sinking fast.

Chapter Nine

Meanwhile, back at the village, everything was in turmoil. As the sun was sinking past the line of trees in the distance, a cry went up from one of the lookout boys.

"Here they come!" he shouted. "I can see the boats of Olaf the Awful and Olga the Awesome. They're on their way across the lake."

Siggy the Big sank down on the ground and covered his face with his big, hairy hands.

"We're doomed," he said. "All is lost."

Helga the Huge stood with her hands on her hips.

"It's your son's fault," she said.

"He's *our* son, actually," muttered Siggy the Big. "You're his Ma, don't forget."

But Helga wasn't listening. "It's all his fault," she went on. "And it's your fault too, Big Sig."

Siggy the Big looked up at her.

"My fault!" he said.

"Yes. If you hadn't agreed to that daft bet we wouldn't be in this mess."

"But it was you . . . " began Siggy the Big.

"Don't try to wheedle your way out of it," retorted Helga the Huge. "If you want me I'll be in having a last look at my longhouse." With a great exaggerated sigh she stormed away.

Siggy the Big groaned again. He wished that the cauldron would come back and that he wouldn't have to hand over his farm to his smartypants brother and his bossyboots wife. But, most of all, he wished his beloved son, Knut, and Sven's precious daughter, Freya, were safely back in the village. Underneath that leather vest, Siggy the Big was just a big softie.

"They're pulling into the fjord," called the lookout. "They've arrived!"

With another great sigh, Siggy the Big got up and went down to the water's edge to hand over his farm, his longhouse and his loyal workers to Olaf the Awful.

Away up on the top of the mountain, Knut and Freya were struggling to get the big, wooden bowl into the nest.

"That's a fine bowl," said the big bird. "And it has no fiddly little jewel bits sticking out of it to catch in my babies' delicate beaks. It's a deal, son. You can have your cauldron back now."

But Knut was shaking his head.

"It's no use," he said. "We're too late. The

sun has almost sunk out of sight. By the time we get down the mountain with the cauldron, my Da will have lost the bet and Olga the Awesome and Olaf the Awful will already have taken over the farm, the longhouse and all the loyal workers. It's no use. We've lost."

"Aw," said the big bird. "Oh well, I'd invite you to stay on here, but, frankly that little girl has been giving me a headache ever since I accidentally picked her up in the cauldron. She keeps going on about the state of the nest and keeps sweeping it out. Has my poor chicks terrified."

"Hmmpff," said Freya.

"Well, see you round, kids," went on the big bird as she lifted the cauldron from the nest in her big talons.

"Let's go, Freya," said Knut sadly. "At least you'll be able to stay on in the village with your Da. I'll have to take to wandering with my Ma and Da."

"Not without you, Knut," said Freya. "I won't stay in the village without you. You're my very best friend."

"That's all very touching," said the big bird. "But if you two wouldn't mind, it's getting a bit crowded in here and I want to settle down for the night. So, cheerio."

Freya looked hard at the big bird. And then she looked thoughtfully at the big bird. And then she spoke.

"You're a fine, big, strong bird," she said.

The big bird preened herself and looked pleased. "Glad you noticed, lass," she said. "I am a pretty fine specimen of birdhood."

"And strong," said Freya.

"And strong," agreed the big bird. "Mega-strong."

"So strong, in fact," went on Freya, "that it would be no bother to you to lift that cauldron, with Knut and me in it, back down to the village. Would it?"

The big bird frowned and looked quite angry.

"She didn't really mean . . . " began Knut.

"Yes, I did," put in Freya, still looking at the big bird. "Will you do it? Please?"

Then the bird's expression changed. She smiled. "Why not?" she said. "After all, Knut has given me this fine bowl which someone will dig up hundreds of years from now and say what a fine craftsman . . . "

"Yeah, yeah," put in Freya. "Let's go. We might just make it if your wings are in full working order."

Just before climbing into the cauldron after Freya, Knut looked at the darkening sky.

"I still don't think we'll make it," he said.

Chapter Ten

Olaf the Awful and Olga the Awesome swaggered up the beach towards Siggy the Big. Behind them a servant struggled to carry something that was wrapped in cloth.

"Probably a seriously valuable thing that will win him the bet," Siggy the Big muttered to his mighty raiders who were standing beside him. "Though, he needn't have bothered. We have nothing to show, so he wins the bet anyway."

"Well, here we are," boomed Olaf the Awful. "Sunset on Thor's Day, like we agreed."

"And we've brought along a seriously valuable thing that my sweet little Olaf picked up on a raid to England," added Olga the Awesome. "What do you have, Brother-in-law?" she added with a snigger. "More sour wine and stinky leather?"

Just then Helga the Huge came out of the longhouse.

"I suppose you think you're going to win this bet?" she said.

"Naturally, pet," replied Olga the Awesome with a smarmy smile. "Have you packed your things? I'd like to move in straight away if you wouldn't mind. I'd like to get my feet up in my new house as soon as possible. These velvet slippers are killing me."

"Let's have a look at your treasure, then," said Olaf the Awful.

"You show us yours first," said Siggy the Big. He was only playing for time, but he knew in his heart that all was lost.

With a dramatic sweep. Olaf the Awful whipped the cloth cover off the treasure.

Everyone gasped.

"A cauldron!" exclaimed Siggy the Big. "Your treasure is a cauldron!"

"A cauldron!" echoed everyone else.

"As fine a cauldron as you'll find anywhere in the world," said Olaf the Awful proudly. And so it was, a pretty fine cauldron.

In fact it was almost identical to the one that Siggy the Big had brought back. Almost.

"Shines up a treat," added Olga the Awesome.

"It's not as nice as my Siggy's cauldron," put in Helga the Huge.

"Oh yeah?" said Olga the Awesome. "So, where is this cauldron then?"

"Big bird flew off with it," muttered Helga the Huge, blushing all the way to the bottom of her neck.

Olaf the Awful and Olga the Awesome fell about laughing.

"Are you trying to tell us . . . " Olaf the Awful paused to wipe the tears of laughter from his eyes. "Are you trying to tell us that you *had* a better cauldron than mine and that some big bird nicked it?"

Siggy the Big nodded, causing Olaf the Awful and Olga the Awesome to fall about laughing again.

"Oh my," said Olaf the Awful. "I've heard hairy excuses in my time, but this is quite the hairiest."

"Or the featheriest," giggled Olga the Awesome.

With that they both collapsed in a fresh bout of laughter.

"It's true," said Helga the Huge. "It was the most magnificent cauldron. It even had shiny bits of jewels around the top."

"I'm sure!" said Olga the Awesome. "Next you'll be telling us it was made of gold."

"It was, it was!" uttered Helga the Huge.

"Look," said Olaf the Awful, his face turning serious. "I haven't time for all this larking about and flimsy excuses. The sun has almost sunk below the lake. You don't have anything to stand up against my cauldron, so hand over, Brother. Your number is up."

Siggy the Big nodded his head sadly. "I suppose you're right," he said. He took a deep breath and signalled to the muttering crowd of villagers to stop muttering. "Brother Olaf the Awful," he said very importantly. "I, Siggy the Big do solemnly hand over my . . . "

But, before he could say another word, a huge shadow fell over the crowd.

"The big bird!" everyone cried, running for cover. From safe hiding-places they watched as the bird hovered for a moment and then, with a great flapping of her huge wings, eased herself down into the middle of the Viking settlement and gently dropped the cauldron on the ground. It wasn't until she had soared back up towards the darkening mountain that the brave Vikings ventured out. As they gingerly approached the cauldron, two small heads popped up.

"Hello there," said Knut.

"Nice to be back. We had a grand flight," said Freya.

Everyone broke into a babble of questions and more questions.

After Knut and Freya told of their big adventure, stopping every so often to be eye-poppingly hugged by Helga the Huge, the cauldron was ceremoniously placed back on its platform. Olaf the Awful's cauldron was placed beside it.

"There's no doubt about it," said Siggy the Big. "Ours is by far a much finer cauldron. But we'll get Sven the Blacksmith to judge. We all know that he is the greatest expert on metal and that he is an honest and fair man because he thinks a lot and likes poetry and stuff like that."

Once more Freya went to fetch her father who was hammering away at his anvil and thinking.

"You're back then," he said to his little daughter. "I'm glad."

"Me too," said Freya. "Now, stop hammering and thinking. There is a very important thing you must do."

Everyone stayed very quiet as Sven the Blacksmith went to where the two cauldrons stood side by side. He scratched his beard and walked around each cauldron. He lifted one and examined it thoroughly. Then he lifted the other.

"Two fine cauldrons," he said eventually.

"Go on then," said Olaf the Awful impatiently. "Which is the better one?"

"Well," said Sven, pointing to Olaf the Awful's cauldron. "This one is a fine piece of work. It's made of copper and is beautifully hand-tooled. See how the plates are rivetted together to give a nice linear pattern. The glassy bits are set in . . . "

"Yes, yes, that's great, Sven," put in Olga. "Look, the sun is almost gone. Get to the important bit. Which cauldron is better?"

Sven nodded and put his hand on the cauldron which the big bird had just delivered.

"This," he said, "is the finest bit of metalwork I've ever seen. This is gold. See how the gold plates are rivetted together in a nice linear pattern and how the crystal stones are set in silver filigree. And, if you look at the handles you'll note the way . . . "

Siggy the Big let Sven wander on. They'd heard enough. Besides, nobody knew what Sven was talking about. The important thing was that Siggy the Big's cauldron was the better piece.

"There you have it, Brother," Siggy the Big smiled. "I've won the bet, fair and square."

Olaf the Awful looked very thunderous. Helga the Huge put her hands on her hips, ready to thump her brother-in-law if he turned awkward.

Then Olaf the Awful smiled. "You're right," he said, as the last of the sun disappeared below the lake. "Fair is fair," he said. "Keep your farm and welcome."

All the Vikings gave a big cheer. Olga the Awesome sniffed. "To think I've brought along my whole wardrobe of hairy frocks and a load of nicked French shoes in preparation for living here," she said.

Helga the Huge beamed proudly at Knut.

"My son," she said, "is one cool Viking."

"*Our* son, actually," muttered Siggy the Big. "I'm his Da, remember?"

But Helga the Huge wasn't listening.

Another banquet was prepared, to which Olaf the Awful and Olga the Awesome were invited, just to show there were no hard feelings. Knut and Freya were allowed to sit at the top table.

"The food is not as smelly up this end," observed Knut.

Siggy the Big told Olaf the Awful about his visit to Ireland.

"Sounds like easy pickings," said Olaf the Awful. "Maybe I'll do a bit of raiding there."

But Knut remembered the promise he and his Da had made to the kind, bald men in the long frocks.

"No, Uncle Olaf!" he exclaimed. "We just barely escaped with our lives. You want to steer clear of those weird people. They have funny haircuts and are very fierce. They're the scariest people you could meet."

"Totally crazy," added Knut's Da, getting carried away. "The meanest, toughest bunch of warriors you'd ever have the misfortune to run into. Do you know, they even pulled our longship out of the water!"

"And one of their tortures is to roast raiders' hands," went on Knut.

"No!" uttered Olaf the Awful. "I'll definitely cross that place off my raid list."

"Anyway, Uncle Olaf," added Knut. "You don't have a longship. That's ours now, remember."

Siggy the Big winked at his son to show how proud he was of him.

After the banquet, the Viking children lifted Knut and Freya shoulder-high and paraded them around the settlement like real celebrities.

"You've sailed away on a raid, you've flown in the air and you've saved your Da's farm," they said. "You can be the leader in our Viking games, Knut."

Knut thought for a moment.

"No thanks, folks," he said. "I've seen it all. I've done the *real* Viking bit so I'd still find your warrior games daft."

"Why can't we all have fun together?" put in Freya. "None of your macho let's-pretend-to-be-Viking nonsense," she added, turning to the other boys. "Something that *all* of us can play."

"Right on, Freya," said the girls.

"Sounds good to me," said Knut. "There's nothing like a bit of fun."

"What about your bowls, Knut?" asked one of the boys. "Some day, hundreds of years from now, someone will dig up your bowls and say what a wonderful craftsman . . . "

"Yeah, yeah," said Knut. "Come on. Let's play."